The Purim Surprise

Lesley Simpson

illustrated by Peter Church

KAR-BEN
PUBLISHING

For my son Ira Reuben, and for the Itkin girls, who gave me my first delivery and taste of shalach manot. —L.S.

To Danielle and Michelle who were such patient models. —P.C.

Text copyright © 2004 by Lesley Simpson
Illustrations copyright © 2004 by Peter Church

KAR-BEN PUBLISHING, INC.
A division of Lerner Publishing Group
241 First Avenue North
Minneapolis, MN 55401 U.S.A.
800-4KARBEN

Website address: www.karben.com

Library of Congress Cataloging-in-Publication Data

Simpson, Lesley.
    The Purim surprise / by Lesley Simpson ; illustrated by Peter Church.
        p.   cm.
    Summary: Having moved to a new city just before Purim, Naomi reluctantly agrees to help deliver shalach manot, Purim treats, to total strangers while worrying that her mother has forgotten her seventh birthday.
    ISBN: 1–58013–090–9 (pbk. : alk. paper)
    [1. Purim—Fiction. 2. Birthdays—Fiction. 3. Moving, Household—Fiction. 4. Jews—United States—Fiction.] I. Church, Peter, ill. II. Title.
PZ7.S6065 Pu 2003
[E]—dc21   2002151696

Manufactured in the United States of America
1 2 3 4 5 6 – JR – 09 08 07 06 05 04

"I think it is a terrible idea," said Naomi.
"I think it will be wonderful," said her mother.

"We don't know anybody," said Naomi.
"We will soon," said her mother.

"We don't know our way around," said Naomi.
"That's why I bought a map," said her mother.

"We'll get lost," said Naomi.
"That's how you get found," said her mother.
"I forgot how to make hamantaschen," said Naomi.
"I have the recipe," said her mom.

"I'm going to hide my face in a paper bag," said Naomi.

"Great idea for a costume," said her mother. "That way I won't have to sew."

"We don't have much time," said Naomi, sitting on a moving box.

Her mom looked at the calendar. Today was Monday. Purim was Thursday. They had just arrived at a new apartment in a new town. Moving boxes were piled from the floor to the ceiling.

"The Passover Haggadah reminds us we were strangers in the land of Egypt," said her mother. "We're strangers today. But not for long."

Her mom had a copy of the town's Jewish directory and was proposing they deliver shalach manot, Purim treats, to total strangers!

Naomi wanted to sink under the floorboards. She wanted to disappear down the bathtub drain. She wanted to hide in a moving box forever.

"You're right. We don't have much time," said her mother. "You'll have to stay up past your bedtime for the next few nights to help me bake."

"Two late nights!" said Naomi. "It's a deal!"

Her mother was usually strict about bedtime. But an important Purim tradition was to turn things upside down.

That morning they didn't unpack. "It's more important to buy candy," said her mom.

They went to the store, but her mom steered the shopping cart past the cucumbers and carrots, straight to the aisle with chocolate bars, lollipops, and watermelon licorice.

"Aren't we going to buy milk?" asked Naomi.
"Only chocolate," said her mom.
"What about breakfast?" asked Naomi.
"Potato chips in cereal bowls," said her mom, giggling.

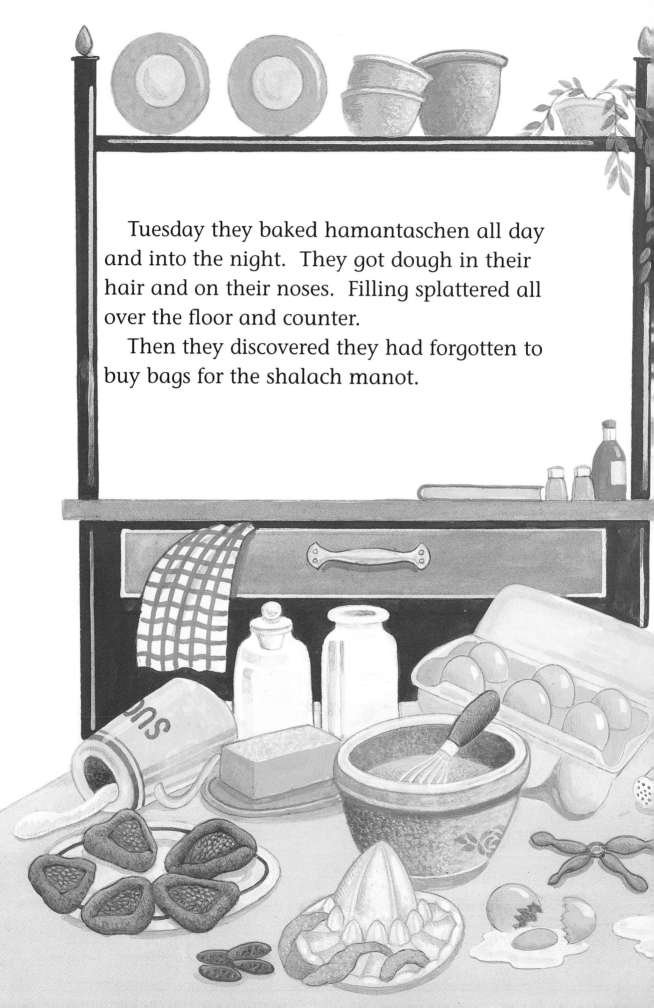

Tuesday they baked hamantaschen all day and into the night. They got dough in their hair and on their noses. Filling splattered all over the floor and counter.

Then they discovered they had forgotten to buy bags for the shalach manot.

"How about these?" said Naomi, holding up a box of ice cream cones.

"Great idea," said her mom. They filled each cone until it overflowed — with peanuts, lollipops, potato chips, lemon drops, and fruit-filled hamantaschen.

Wednesday evening they listened to the Megillah reading at the synagogue. For her costume, Naomi put a brown grocery bag over her head, so nobody would know who she was. Her mom dressed as the Queen of Hearts.

As they walked home, Naomi felt miserable. The next day was her birthday and her mom hadn't said a word about it. She felt warm tears fall on her cheeks and onto the bag. How could your own mother forget your birthday?

It was still dark Thursday morning when they began their Purim deliveries. They tucked cones with shalach manot into empty flowerpots on windowsills, propped them up in hammocks, and hid them in bicycle and tricycle baskets.

Ahuva Gold found a cone inside her double stroller.

Esther Brown discovered one near her birdhouse in the dogwood tree.

Harry Marks found one inside his motorcycle helmet.

Sophia Gershon found hers peeking between the newspapers in her recycling box.

They licked lollipops together while they studied the map. They got lost nine times. By the end of the day every address in the Jewish directory had received Purim treats.

Because they were new in town,
they didn't know Max and Michael
Saltzman were fighting.

They didn't know that folks were terrified
of Mrs. Fish because she growled at her
customers. They didn't know that the
Shapiros were no longer speaking to the
Kaplans. Everyone mattered, her mother
said. Everyone got shalach manot.

Inside, however,
Naomi was feeling
sad. Her mother
still had said
nothing about her
birthday.

But there was something Naomi didn't know.

Naomi's mom had tucked a secret
invitation into each gift of shalach manot.

It read:

Don your costume, polish your crown
Come and meet us, we're new in town.
Bring your flute, fiddle or drum
And join us for some Purim fun.
We'll sing and dance and celebrate
And nosh on chocolate birthday cake...

For here's a secret — Naomi Levin
On Purim Day is turning seven!

—From Ruth Levin (Naomi's mom)
30 Bond Street, Apartment 3

When they got home, Naomi went into her bedroom and closed the door. She cried into her pillow until it was soggy, then turned the pillow over to the dry side and cried harder.

She was whispering her problems to her teddy bear when she heard a commotion right outside the door.

There was singing, cheering, laughing, and applause. She peeked into the living room.

The apartment door was open and a colorful parade snaked down the hallway and around the corner. Everyone was in costume, and everyone was carrying something.

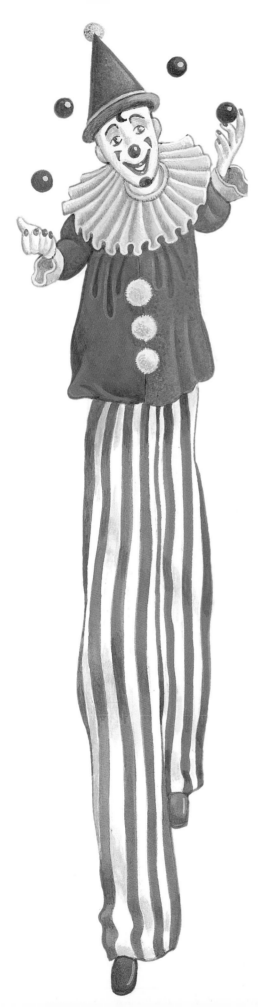

Queen Esther, in her jeweled crown, brought a huge bunch of balloons. A clown on stilts juggled colorful balls. The cantor, dressed as a king in purple robes, was followed by masked musicians playing their instruments. One by one they came inside.

"Happy Purim, and thanks for the shalach manot," they said as they introduced themselves. Soon the apartment was overflowing with people . . . and soccer balls, badminton racquets, and treasure maps. Someone dressed as Vashti brought a dress-up trunk overflowing with crowns, gowns, and scarves.

The butcher pulled magic cards from his vest and began to do tricks. The rabbi brought stories in his head and told them to anyone who would listen. An artist set up an easel on the balcony and began drawing caricatures. Someone was playing guitar in the shower.

A juggler led Naomi into the room and placed a gold crown on her head.

The butcher handed out party hats,
noise-makers, and sparklers. Naomi's
mom brought out a birthday cake, and
the cantor took out his baton and led
everyone in singing "Happy Birthday."
And everyone knew Naomi's name.

Naomi took the biggest breath
she could and closed her eyes.
She made a wish and blew out
the flames on her birthday
candles.

Her mom was right, thought Naomi. They were strangers no more.

About Purim

Purim is a joyous holiday celebrated in the spring. It commemorates the victory of the Jews against wicked Haman, the advisor to the Persian king Ahashuerus. The story, which is retold in the Biblical book of Esther, is read in synagogue from a scroll called a megillah. It is customary to twirl noisemakers (groggers) when the villain's name is read. Purim is celebrated with costume parades, feasting, and the exchange of sweet Purim treats (shalach manot).

Glossary

Haman—the villain of the Purim story
Hamantaschen—three-cornered filled cookies often included in shalach manot baskets
Megillah—the Biblical book of Esther read on Purim
Passover Haggadah—the book containing the story of the Exodus and prayers and rituals used at the Passover seder
Queen Esther—the heroine of the Purim story
Shalach Manot—gifts of food exchanged among family and friends
Vashti—the queen banished by King Ahashuerus in the Purim story

About the author and illustrator

Lesley Simpson is the author of *The Shabbat Box* (Kar-Ben) and *The Hug* (Annick Press), which she also illustrated. As a journalist for a Hamilton, Ontario, daily newspaper, she works writing grown-up stories. She especially loves the Purim tradition of shalach manot and has a soft spot for sweets.

Peter Church is a freelance artist who illustrates a variety of educational children's books. He was born in Reading, near London, England, where he studied art and worked in a design studio. He moved to the U.S. in 1985 and lives near Worcester, MA, with his wife Mary and two sons.